A School – for Girls!

Stories linking with the History
National Curriculum Key Stage 2

First published in 1999 by Franklin Watts
96 Leonard Street, London EC2A 4XD

Editor: Sarah Snashall
Designer: Jason Anscomb
Consultant: Dr Anne Millard, BA Hons, Dip Ed, PhD

A CIP catalogue record for this book
is available from the British Library.

ISBN   0 7496 3360 3 (hbk)
         0 7496 3549 5 (pbk)

Dewey Classification 941.081

Printed in Great Britain

ROTHERHAM LIBRARY & INFORMATION SERVICES

This book must be returned by the date specified at the time of issue
as the DATE DUE FOR RETURN.
The loan may be extended (personally, by post or telephone) for a
further period if the book is not required by another reader, by quoting
the above number / author / title.

LIS7a

A School – for Girls!

by
Natalie Grice

Illustrations by Kate Sheppard

W
FRANKLIN WATTS
NEW YORK • LONDON • SYDNEY

1
Birthday news

It happened at tea-time on our birthday.

"Happy birthday, Artie. Happy birthday, Annie. I hope you liked your presents." Father smiled at me. "Have you thought of a name for your doll yet, Annie?"

"Em – not yet, Father." I didn't say I

would rather have had books. Dolls were for little girls, not twelve-year-olds. I preferred to read, or have play-fights with

 Artie's toy soldiers – although more often than not, they turned into real fights with him. My twin brother and I never admitted defeat – especially not against each other.

"You'll be able to make little clothes for it," said Mother.

I groaned silently. I hated sewing.

That was the worst thing about being a girl. Sewing. Artie never had to do needlework. Or any domestic work. I had argued till I was blue in the face about this. All my parents ever said was, it was my DUTY to do it. They never said why it wasn't Artie's duty. That was one of the reasons I enjoyed going to Miss Franklin's morning school so much. At least there the boys and girls did the same lessons.

But as today was a celebration, I didn't make my usual complaint, even though I could see Artie smirking on the other side of the dining table. I kicked him hard on the shins. That wiped the smile off his face!

Father turned to Artie as he was gingerly rubbing his leg.

"Well, my boy," he began, "today is a big day for you."

"Er – yes, Father," Artie answered doubtfully. I felt a bit put out. It was my birthday too.

Father continued, "You know, I've been in the drapery business for thirty years. I started as an lowly apprentice in 1820. And now look at me. I've got my own business. You're lucky, Artie. You've

8

got your future all mapped out. You'll be working for me one day."

Both Artie and I started to fidget. Father could be such a bore about the linen drapery shop he ran from the front

rooms of our house. We exchanged one of our 'here he goes again' looks. There were a few things we agreed on.

"I want you to be well prepared for it. So, from tomorrow, you will be attending

Livermore's Grammar School for Young Men. Your mother has made your uniform, and I have bought the necessary books." Father gave a pleased little smile at Artie. "Well, boy? What do you think of your birthday surprise?"

Artie's look of shock, mirroring the one on my face, was instantly replaced by a smooth smile.

"It's wonderful, Father. Thank you," he said quickly.

Mother took his hand. "My dear son. We know you'll make us proud of you."

Nobody noticed me turning purple in the corner. Eventually I managed to splutter, "Um – where am I going to, Father?"

He and Mother both looked puzzled. I tried to be clearer. "What school will I be attending?"

Mother laughed. "School? You don't need any more schooling. You need to improve your sewing and learn to cook.

This week you'll be going to Aunt Mary's to help her make new curtains. She doesn't know you're coming yet. Won't it be a nice surprise for her?"

I couldn't believe my ears. Artie was going to grammar school – and I was going to make curtains?

My chair fell over as I shot to my feet. "That's not fair!" I screeched. "I'm just as clever as Artie. You know I am. I could work in the business too. I hate cooking! I hate sewing! I'm no good at them." I grabbed Father by the arm. "Please send me to school, please!" I begged.

"Anna!" my mother exclaimed. She only called me Anna when I was in trouble, which was most of the time. "Sit down this instant!" I ignored her.

"Father, you know I love school lessons. Please – "

"Anna!" he said. "Do as your mother says. The only lessons you need are in how a young lady should behave."

"I'm not a young lady," I shouted, still standing.

"No, but you will be," Father said firmly. "And a young lady does what she's told without arguing. Ladies don't go to school or to work, they look after their husbands

and children. Now go to your room."

I flew to the door, but turned and said, "I can do anything Artie can – just you watch!" And before they could say anything, I slammed the door behind me and ran sobbing to my room.

2
Off to Aunt Mary's

It was early the next morning and I was on my way to Aunt Mary's house. She was my great-aunt, was about 200 years old (all right, she was 60 really) and was the strictest, meanest person I knew. I was terrified of her. She ate children for breakfast – at least, I was convinced she did. That's another way Artie was lucky. She couldn't stand little boys, so he never had to visit her.

I was trudging along, head down, feeling very sorry for myself, when I overheard a girl's voice say, "Come on Louisa, we don't want to be late for school on the first day."

School? I looked up. Two girls were walking just in front of me. One was about

my age and size. The other was taller and probably a year or two older. They were both carrying small bags.

The tall one spoke. "I hope Miss Buss won't be too strict with us."

"So do I, Grace," answered the shorter one, who must have been Louisa. "My last teacher used to slap our hands if we gave the wrong answer!"

The girls crossed the street. Without thinking, I followed. They continued to

discuss this Miss Buss and how nervous they were. At the end of the street, they turned right. Aunt Mary's house was a few streets away – to the left.

I hesitated. Aunt Mary wasn't expecting me so I couldn't really be late. And it wouldn't hurt just to take a look at this school …

The girls had reached the end of the street and were turning the corner. They'd disappear if I dallied any longer. That made my mind up for me. I pelted down the street, then peeked carefully round the corner. Where were they? I'd lost them! No, there they were, nearly out of sight behind a carriage. Keeping the carriage between them and me, I snaked my way down the street, making sure they didn't see me. In this and other ridiculous ways, I tailed the girls for ten minutes.

Finally, we came to a road called Camden Street. A group of girls had congregated outside number 46. Louisa and Grace stood at the edge of it, exchanging nervous glances with some of the others. I stood a little way down the road watching expectantly.

A church bell chimed out nine o'clock. When the last 'dong' had faded, the front door opened. The girls started to file in. As the last two were stepping through the door, I threw caution and common sense to the wind, and ran in after them.
I was inside Miss Buss's school!

3
Miss Buss

We were directed into a large airy room by
a middle-aged woman who told us Miss
Buss would be with us in a minute. Most
of the girls stood around the edges of the
room, looking ill-at-ease with their
surroundings. A few of the bolder ones had

taken seats at desks dotted around the room. I was too dazed by what I had done to feel either nervous or brave.

Until I heard footsteps approaching… Then suddenly, my legs turned to jelly. What was I doing? I was in this house without being invited. Father said that people who were in your house without an invitation were burglars. And burglars went to jail or were even – gulp – hanged!

There was no time to lose. The door started to open. All the girls were watching eagerly to see their new teacher. I looked around wildly. There was a door behind

me. I turned the handle. It wasn't locked. I stumbled into a book-filled cupboard. I was safe – for now.

"Good morning, girls," a voice said. "Please take a seat." I heard the rustling of clothes against wood. "That's better. I'm so glad to see you all here this morning, my dears. My name is Frances Mary Buss, and I am the headmistress of our new school, the North London

Collegiate School for Ladies. I hope that together we will make a success of it."

A school for ladies? Father was wrong then – ladies DID go to school.

Miss Buss began to call out names. The girls answered, 'Here, Miss Buss' or 'Yes, Ma'am'. I heard the names Louisa Benson and Grace Elliot called.

"Caroline Waters." There was no response. "Caroline Waters? Does anyone know Caroline Waters?" Nobody spoke. "We'll have to begin without her," said Miss Buss. "I'll get out the books."

Books? These books? I was done for! I crouched down at the back of the cupboard in a hopeless effort to hide.

The door opened. Light streamed in, blinding me for a moment. When the spots before my eyes cleared I saw a young woman with an anxious look on her face bending over me.

"Heavens above!" she exclaimed. "What has happened to you? Why are you in here? Have you fainted?"

I stared up at her dumbly, not able to move a muscle.

The anxious look was slowly replaced by a frown.

"What are you doing here? Who are you?" she asked.

In a panic, I said the first thing that came into my head.

"Please, Miss Buss," I gabbled, "I'm Caroline Waters."

4
School

The day went by in a blur. In the morning
we studied grammar, took a quick tour
around the British Isles in geography, and
started French lessons. I learnt to say
what sounded like 'Sher-ma-pell Caroline'
which meant 'My name is Caroline' in

French – even though, of course, it wasn't.

But the best thing of all was the last lesson of the day. Miss Buss went to the blackboard and wrote six strange words on it: Amo, Amas, Amat, Amamus, Amatis, Amant.

"Does anybody know what these words mean?" she asked.

Silence.

"Does anybody know what language this is?"

Still nobody replied.

"This, girls, is Latin, the language the Romans spoke to each other two thousand years ago," Miss Buss said.

The language the Romans spoke? And we were still learning it today, in 1850? Wow!

"These words form the verb 'to love'." I couldn't remember what a verb was but that didn't matter. I was learning Roman speech.

"They mean, in order – 'I love', 'you love', 'he or she loves', 'we love', 'you love' (when speaking to more than one person), and 'they love'," she explained.

By the end of the lesson, I knew them off by heart. I couldn't believe it. I was in school, doing just what Artie was doing. Well, I'd said I could do anything he could!

At three o'clock, Miss Buss said, "That'll be all for today, girls. Caroline, may I see you for a moment?"

My blood turned cold.

The others left. I shuffled up to her desk.

"Have I done something wrong, Miss Buss?" I asked nervously.

She smiled warmly. "Not at all, my dear. You've done very well today. I think you have the makings of an excellent student."

I blushed with pleasure. If I could

just keep coming to the school for a bit longer I'd show her that she was right!

"There's just one thing," she continued. "I haven't received your fees yet."

"Fees?" I repeated stupidly.

"Yes, fees. You know, to pay for the classes. Perhaps the letter got lost in the post." She handed me an envelope. "There's a bill in here. Could you tell your father payment must be made by the end of the month. I'll see you tomorrow."

I trudged out of the class in a daze. How could I

have been so stupid? Of course there'd be fees. What was I going to do now?

I had a month. Somehow, I'd work it out before then.

When I got home the first thing I did was hide the envelope in my toy box. I hardly ever opened it now, so it was sure to be safe.

At supper that evening, Artie was bragging to Father and Mother about all

the things he'd done in school. I had to pinch myself to stop myself from laughing. If only they knew!

"... and in Latin we learnt to how to say 'I love', 'you love' and so on. Shall I show you? Amo, amas, amat, amamus, amatis, amad."

He sat back, looking unbearably smug.

"Actually," I said quietly, "it's amant, not amad."

Artie opened and shut his mouth like a flabbergasted goldfish. He looked so stupid. That'd teach him to be a show-off. Then he looked at me accusingly.

"All right, Miss Clever. Just where did you learn Latin?"

What had I done? Mother and Father were looking at me curiously.

"I – er –" I stammered, "I – found it in a book."

"Oh yeah?" Artie said disbelievingly. "Show me."

I thought quickly. "I can't show you because it's at Aunt Mary's house."

"Aunt Mary's?" he sneered. "There's no Latin books there."

"How would you know?" I cried, my cheeks turning scarlet. "You've never even been there! I found it today in a box."

"You're lying," he muttered again. A funny look came into his eyes. "And I'm going to prove it."

5
Artie gets suspicious

At breakfast the next morning, Artie watched me carefully, no doubt wondering why I wasn't scowling fiercely at everybody. I tried to look a bit miserable, but it's very difficult when you know you're putting one over on your nearest and dearest.

I finished my breakfast and smiled sweetly at Mother. "I'll be off then. Aunt Mary will be expecting me."

"Hold on a moment, Annie," Artie said quickly, a sly look on his face.

"Auntie's house is near my school, isn't it? I could keep you company on the way – make sure you get there safely."

"What a good idea, Artie," said Mother. "I'm glad to see you thinking of your sister. You're becoming a proper little gentleman."

He was up to something. But if I objected to walking with him, he'd be even more suspicious. I had to beat him at his own game.

"Come on then," I said and frowned convincingly. "Aunt Mary will only complain if I'm late."

In the street, Artie said, "You're gonna show me that Latin book when we get there."

So that was what he was after. This was turning into a nightmare. If I went to Aunt Mary's, Artie would find out there

was no book. But worse than that, I'd never be able to go to school again. Of course, Artie didn't know the way to Aunt Mary's on his own ...

"Is that all you can think about?" I scoffed. "You just can't bear knowing you're not better than me at anything."

"Oh yes, I am!"

"Oh no, you're not"

"I am too! I'm brainier, faster and stronger than you," he cried.

"Oh yes?" I took a quick look along the street. The gas lampposts caught my eye. "Alright then, prove it," I challenged. "First one to the top of a lamppost is the best."

"You're on!"

We ran to the posts and started climbing. I could see Artie puffing and panting in his effort to beat me. We both reached the middle at the same time. He had his back to me. I let go and dropped to the ground. Artie carried on climbing. I watched him pull his way to the top. He

looked at my lamppost only to see me grinning up at him from its base.

"Have a nice day at school, brother dear. Don't be late now," I called. I spun on my heel and pelted down the road, only stopping when I was about four streets away. Then I collapsed on the ground and laughed so much that tears poured down my cheeks.

A church clock struck quarter to nine. I stood up, wiped my eyes and started walking. I had to get to school on time too!

6

A second day at school

Miss Buss looked at the clock.

"Home-time, girls."

My second day of school was over.
Today we had started doing history, and I
now knew all the kings and queens of
England since 1066. I had memorized the

complete list, and Miss Buss had given me a peppermint as a prize. I recited the names in my mind as I walked home, sucking on my sweet. "William the Conqueror, William the Second, Henry the First, Stephen, Henry the Second, Richard the Lionheart ..."

When I got home, I expected Artie to get me for the trick I'd played on him. But he wasn't anywhere to be seen. All the better for me. I went up to my bedroom and pretended to be Miss Buss teaching the class. But I didn't have anyone to teach. Then I thought of my dolls. They would make ideal pupils – they sat still, didn't interrupt and never asked questions the teacher couldn't answer.

I went over to my toy box, but stopped short. The catch on the box was open. I had closed it tightly yesterday after hiding the letter in it. My heart started thumping. By the time I had pulled out every doll onto the floor and turned the box upside down, it sounded as loud as the chimes of Big Ben! No envelope. Only one person could have taken it. Artie! He must have been looking for that imaginary Latin book.

I ran into his bedroom. Where would he have put it? I went through every drawer in his cabinet like a whirlwind. Clothes, toys, and bits of paper went flying everywhere.

"Lost something, Annie?" enquired a voice as I was bending over waist-deep

into a smelly laundry basket.

I jumped up. Artie was leaning on the doorframe looking extremely amused.

"Yes – um – no, not me, nothing, I just, I – er," I garbled.

"Sorry Annie, I didn't quite understand that," said Artie, with an evil smile from ear to ear.

"I – that is, Mother asked me to look for something she thinks she might have dropped in one of our rooms," I lied. Would he fall for it?

No chance. "Something she dropped, eh?" he said, as if talking to an idiot. "A hanky maybe? A hairpin?"

"Em – no," I hedged.

"Maybe it was a recipe. Or a shopping list," he suggested.

"It was an envelope," I squeaked.

"An envelope?" he repeated. "No,

haven't seen one of those in here.
Sorry sis."

I was defeated for the moment. I started to walk past him out of the room.

"Funnily enough, though, I did see one in your room. You needn't worry about looking any more. I've just given it to Father."

A spinning top couldn't turn faster than I did. "You swine!" I squealed. "I'm going to kill you Artie Foster"

And for the millionth time in our lives, Artie and I fell to the floor and tried to choke each other to death.

7
Curtains

"Ow!" I cried as I jabbed my finger with the needle for the hundredth time that day. "I hate sewing!"

It was all over – no more Latin classes, kings of England, or Miss Buss. Mother and Father had dragged the whole story out of me. As you can imagine, they weren't best pleased. My punishment was to sit in the stockroom behind Father's shop, sewing – guess what? – new curtains for Aunt Mary's house. They said they didn't trust me to go out of their sight. I'd been there for three days. It seemed like a lifetime.

"How are you, Annie?"

I groaned. It was Artie, back from school. He swaggered into the stockroom.

"Or shall I say it in French? Com-ment-a-lay-voo, Annie?" He grinned. "Now, have I said that right? Oh, I forgot. You're not learning French any more. How silly of me. Never mind. I see the curtains are coming along well."

One step closer and he'd have this needle in his chubby backside!

Just then, Mother called him to come and have some cake. Luckily for me, he was a pig for anything sweet. He ran off without another word.

I was left alone with my sore finger and heavy heart. Artie knew just how to get me where it hurt without using a needle.

The shop doorbell tinkled. "Good afternoon, Madam," I heard my father say. "How may I be of assistance?"

"Good afternoon," a woman replied. I looked up. That voice – where did I know it from?

She continued, "I'd like to look at some fabric."

Oh my stars! I suddenly knew where

I'd heard that voice. I went running into
the shop.

"Miss Buss!" I cried.

"Caroline!" she exclaimed. "Why
haven't you been in school?"

"Caroline?" said Father.

"Yes, Caroline," repeated Miss Buss.

"Her name's Annie," said Father.

They both looked at me. "Caroline?" said Miss Buss.

I took a deep breath. "My name's not Caroline," I confessed. "It's Annie Foster." I started to babble. "I didn't mean to lie to you but I wanted to go to school and be as good as Artie at everything, and I loved it so much I had to keep on pretending to be Caroline – "

"Annie," Miss Buss interrupted, "You've lost me already. Start again at the beginning."

So the whole story came tumbling out. Artie starting school, Aunt Mary's, following the girls, how unfairly I'd been treated ... Father's face turned a funny colour at that point. I quickly shut up.

"So," he said to Miss Buss. "You're the little lady who's been filling my daughter's head with nonsense."

"Nonsense?" she repeated, just as quietly as before. It was impossible to imagine Miss Buss shouting. "Do you think it's nonsense for a girl to be sensibly educated rather than have an empty mind and be of no use to anyone?"

Father's face was a picture. He had never heard a woman speak like this to him. Miss Buss looked at me.

"You should be extremely proud of Annie. She is one of the brightest pupils I've ever taught. She's obviously desperate to be educated. Don't you think she deserves a chance?"

Father frowned at the floor.

A canny expression crossed Miss Buss's face. "Mr Foster," she said, "I was going to place an order for material for my sewing classes. It's a very big order," she stressed. Father suddenly looked up. "In fact, if the school is successful, I'll need a constant supply. But maybe I should go to another draper. I can see you don't wish to talk to me."

She'd got his attention now! I could almost see the fear in Father's eyes as he imagined the order going to a rival shop.

"Now, let's not be too hasty," he said quickly. "I have to admit, I've never thought much about Annie's mind. But she certainly seems keen on your school. Maybe I haven't been fair ..."

Father glanced in my direction. I fixed my gaze on him and watched him slowly weaken.

"As from Monday," he pronounced, "Annie will be attending school."

I gasped with delight and threw my arms around his waist. "Thank you, Father."

Miss Buss beamed. Father turned to her. "And you'll be able to send any orders you have home with her," he said.

I didn't care how it had happened – I was going to school!

And Artie was going to be the first to know!

Victorian Education

Schools for the lucky

There was no state education in the 19th century. There were schools for the few rich children whose parents could afford the fees. And, in some places there were schools provided for free for the children of the village by a wealthy landowner or the church. Some charged a small fee to cover the cost of paying the teacher. Usually, one teacher taught the whole school, with pupils aged from four up to about fourteen!

It wasn't until 1870 that primary education was organised throughout the whole country to try and provide every child with a school place. In 1918, primary education was made free.

Education for girls

Many people in Victorian times didn't think women were strong enough to be able to learn very much. In fact, they thought too much education could make them ill! Too much education was also seen as being 'unladylike'.

SWOON

Miss Buss

Miss Buss was a real person. In 1850 she opened
The North London Collegiate School for Ladies.
This school still exists today.

Miss Buss, a young woman of 23, wanted to
provide girls with a proper secondary education.
Miss Buss felt that the few schools that did offer

teaching to older girls were not doing it properly. A lot of them concentrated on "parrot fashion" learning, without teaching the girls to really think about what they were learning.

The school was unusual for its time because it admitted girls from very different social backgrounds. Normally, different social

classes were kept strictly apart. The school was so successful that it was used as a model for other girls' schools set up in later years. Miss Buss is still remembered today for the important work she did in starting proper education for women.

Sparks: Historical Adventures

ANCIENT GREECE
The Great Horse of Troy – The Trojan War
0 7496 3369 7 (hbk) 0 7496 3538 X (pbk)
The Winner's Wreath – Ancient Greek Olympics
0 7496 3368 9 (hbk) 0 7496 3555 X (pbk)

INVADERS AND SETTLERS
Boudicca Strikes Back – The Romans in Britain
0 7496 3366 2 (hbk) 0 7496 3546 0 (pbk)
Viking Raiders – A Norse Attack
0 7496 3089 2 (hbk) 0 7496 3457 X (pbk)
Erik's New Home – A Viking Town
0 7496 3367 0 (hbk) 0 7496 3552 5 (pbk)
TALES OF THE ROWDY ROMANS
The Great Necklace Hunt
0 7496 2221 0 (hbk) 0 7496 2628 3 (pbk)
The Lost Legionary
0 7496 2222 9 (hbk) 0 7496 2629 1 (pbk)
The Guard Dog Geese
0 7496 2331 4 (hbk) 0 7496 2630 5 (pbk)
A Runaway Donkey
0 7496 2332 2 (hbk) 0 7496 2631 3 (pbk)

TUDORS AND STUARTS
Captain Drake's Orders – The Armada
0 7496 2556 2 (hbk) 0 7496 3121 X (pbk)
London's Burning – The Great Fire of London
0 7496 2557 0 (hbk) 0 7496 3122 8 (pbk)
Mystery at the Globe – Shakespeare's Theatre
0 7496 3096 5 (hbk) 0 7496 3449 9 (pbk)
Plague! – A Tudor Epidemic
0 7496 3365 4 (hbk) 0 7496 3556 8 (pbk)
Stranger in the Glen – Rob Roy
0 7496 2586 4 (hbk) 0 7496 3123 6 (pbk)
A Dream of Danger – The Massacre of Glencoe
0 7496 2587 2 (hbk) 0 7496 3124 4 (pbk)
A Queen's Promise – Mary Queen of Scots
0 7496 2589 9 (hbk) 0 7496 3125 2 (pbk)
Over the Sea to Skye – Bonnie Prince Charlie
0 7496 2588 0 (hbk) 0 7496 3126 0 (pbk)
TALES OF A TUDOR TEARAWAY
A Pig Called Henry
0 7496 2204 4 (hbk) 0 7496 2625 9 (pbk)
A Horse Called Deathblow
0 7496 2205 9 (hbk) 0 7496 2624 0 (pbk)
Dancing for Captain Drake
0 7496 2234 2 (hbk) 0 7496 2626 7 (pbk)
Birthdays are a Serious Business
0 7496 2235 0 (hbk) 0 7496 2627 5 (pbk)

VICTORIAN ERA
The Runaway Slave – The British Slave Trade
0 7496 3093 0 (hbk) 0 7496 3456 1 (pbk)
The Sewer Sleuth – Victorian Cholera
0 7496 2590 2 (hbk) 0 7496 3128 7 (pbk)
Convict! – Criminals Sent to Australia
0 7496 2591 0 (hbk) 0 7496 3129 5 (pbk)
An Indian Adventure – Victorian India
0 7496 3090 6 (hbk) 0 7496 3451 0 (pbk)
Farewell to Ireland – Emigration to America
0 7496 3094 9 (hbk) 0 7496 3448 0 (pbk)

The Great Hunger – Famine in Ireland
0 7496 3095 7 (hbk) 0 7496 3447 2 (pbk)
Fire Down the Pit – A Welsh Mining Disaster
0 7496 3091 4 (hbk) 0 7496 3450 2 (pbk)
Tunnel Rescue – The Great Western Railway
0 7496 3353 0 (hbk) 0 7496 3537 1 (pbk)
Kidnap on the Canal – Victorian Waterways
0 7496 3352 2 (hbk) 0 7496 3540 1 (pbk)
Dr. Barnardo's Boys – Victorian Charity
0 7496 3358 1 (hbk) 0 7496 3541 X (pbk)
The Iron Ship – Brunel's Great Britain
0 7496 3355 7 (hbk) 0 7496 3543 6 (pbk)
Bodies for Sale – Victorian Tomb-Robbers
0 7496 3364 6 (hbk) 0 7496 3539 8 (pbk)
Penny Post Boy – The Victorian Postal Service
0 7496 3362 X (hbk) 0 7496 3544 4 (pbk)
The Canal Diggers – The Manchester Ship Canal
0 7496 3356 5 (hbk) 0 7496 3545 2 (pbk)
The Tay Bridge Tragedy – A Victorian Disaster
0 7496 3354 9 (hbk) 0 7496 3547 9 (pbk)
Stop, Thief! – The Victorian Police
0 7496 3359 X (hbk) 0 7496 3548 7 (pbk)
A School – for Girls! – Victorian Schools
0 7496 3360 3 (hbk) 0 7496 3549 5 (pbk)
Chimney Charlie – Victorian Chimney Sweeps
0 7496 3351 4 (hbk) 0 7496 3551 7 (pbk)
Down the Drain – Victorian Sewers
0 7496 3357 3 (hbk) 0 7496 3550 9 (pbk)
The Ideal Home – A Victorian New Town
0 7496 3361 1 (hbk) 0 7496 3553 3 (pbk)
Stage Struck – Victorian Music Hall
0 7496 3363 8 (hbk) 0 7496 3554 1 (pbk)
TRAVELS OF A YOUNG VICTORIAN
The Golden Key
0 7496 2360 8 (hbk) 0 7496 2632 1 (pbk)
Poppy's Big Push
0 7496 2361 6 (hbk) 0 7496 2633 X (pbk)
Poppy's Secret
0 7496 2374 8 (hbk) 0 7496 2634 8 (pbk)
The Lost Treasure
0 7496 2375 6 (hbk) 0 7496 2635 6 (pbk)

20th-CENTURY HISTORY
Fight for the Vote – The Suffragettes
0 7496 3092 2 (hbk) 0 7496 3452 9 (pbk)
The Road to London – The Jarrow March
0 7496 2609 7 (hbk) 0 7496 3132 5 (pbk)
The Sandbag Secret – The Blitz
0 7496 2608 9 (hbk) 0 7496 3133 3 (pbk)
Sid's War – Evacuation
0 7496 3209 7 (hbk) 0 7496 3445 6 (pbk)
D-Day! – Wartime Adventure
0 7496 3208 9 (hbk) 0 7496 3446 4 (pbk)
The Prisoner – A Prisoner of War
0 7496 3212 7 (hbk) 0 7496 3455 3 (pbk)
Escape from Germany – Wartime Refugees
0 7496 3211 9 (hbk) 0 7496 3454 5 (pbk)
Flying Bombs – Wartime Bomb Disposal
0 7496 3210 0 (hbk) 0 7496 3453 7 (pbk)
12,000 Miles From Home – Sent to Australia
0 7496 3370 0 (hbk) 0 7496 3542 8 (pbk)